CW01582665

Ama and The Lost Key

WRITTEN BY:

Sarah Kittoe

Illustrated by Jason Lee

Conscious Dreams
PUBLISHING

Ama and the Lost Key

Copyright © 2024 Sarah Kittoe

All rights reserved. No part of this publication may be produced, distributed, or transmitted in any form or by any means, including photocopying, recording, or other electronic or mechanical methods, without the prior written permission of the publisher, except in the case of brief quotations embodied in critical reviews and certain other non-commercial uses permitted by copyright law.

First Printed in United Kingdom 2024

Published by Conscious Dreams Publishing
www.consciousdreamspublishing.com

Illustrated by Jason Lee

Edited by Elise Abram

Typeset by Bryony Dick

ISBN: 978-1-915522-63-4

Dedication

To my little sister, Mary Kittoe, you will always be my best friend.
To Mummy and Daddy, thank you for your love and support always.

M & K

Hi, I am Ama. I live in Ghana, which is in West Africa. I was born and raised there, and it is a beautiful country full of adventures, but last week was the most exciting or should I say mysterious week of my life.

Let me explain.

Last Monday, I was walking home from school when I spotted something shiny on the ground. I made my way over to pick it up, thinking that it was my lucky day as I had found a coin to add to my savings, but I was wrong. When I picked it up, I saw that it was a key made of pure gold.

I was astonished. 'What is a gold key doing on this dusty floor, and how did it get there?' I said in shock.

The key looked precious and valuable, and I couldn't wait to get home to do some research about it. I was sure I would find something about it, as it had the initials 'NK & AK' on it. I wondered what the initials stood for and who might have lost such precious key, and a thrill of excitement rushed through my body.

I had a mystery to solve.

Eager to Know More About the Key

I rushed to my room and switched on my computer as soon as I got home. It was then I heard a firm voice calling my name.

"AMA!" It was my mother. She must have heard me rush upstairs to my room without greeting her when I got home.

'Yes, Mummy,' I responded, making my way downstairs.
'Good afternoon, Mummy,' I said when I saw her. 'You called me?'

'What is the rush? You flew in here as if you were being chased by lions. Is everything okay?' Mum asked with a concerned look.

'Yes, all is well, Ma. I just have this research I need to get started on,' I responded, staring at the floor.

'You know you have your afternoon work to do first before going upstairs. Please, the chickens and goats need feeding, and can you pick the ripe mangoes before the birds get to them?' Mum asked as she continued chopping the vegetables.

'Yes, Ma. I will get it done right away,' I said, and I went off to do the chores. I wanted to get them done as soon as possible so I could solve the mystery.

Feeding the goats and chickens had always been my favourite job. I love seeing how the animals get on so well together. It helps me get on well with people regardless of who they are or how they look. I also enjoy chasing the goats around. They can be stubborn but fun to be around them. Although they tend to chew on your clothes and shoes, it is like having a lot of pets to play with. When I finished feeding the goats and chickens, I went to the backyard to pick the ripe mangoes. That year was a fruitful season as the mangoes flourished. I was able to smell the exotic, succulent fruit from afar.

When I finally finished with my chores, I rushed back to my room and got the mysterious golden key with the 'NK & AK' initials out of my drawer. I turned on my computer and started the research to see what I could find.

I did some research on my computer. I discovered something interesting. The key belonged to a South African lady called Nombuso.

Who was she? If she was South African, then how did her key get to Ghana?

It was getting late, and still, I had several questions that needed answering if I was going to solve this mystery. My parents liked to pray and read with me before going to bed, so I decided to get ready for bed and continue with my research the next day.

Teamwork Time

The next morning, I was awoken by the crow of the rooster outside: 'Cock-a-doodle-doo!' The rooster's crow was my alarm. On a normal day, I cover my head with my blanket and refuse to wake up, but that morning, I knew I had an adventure to research.

I got up and got ready for my day, excited to share my findings with my friends.

When I got to school, I met up with Afua, Mpume and Thatho, who were my best friends. We had been friends since nursery, and we were known as 'The Friendship Club'. I told them about the key and took it out of my pocket to show them.

'Wow! That's amazing!' Afua exclaimed.

'Look at the type of writing on it. I have never seen such cursive style before,' said Mpume.

'The key looks precious. I am sure it's valuable to the owner. I wonder how it got lost. I am sure the owner has been looking for it. Do you know who it belongs to?' Thatho asked.

'Well, last night, I found out that it belongs to a woman called Nombuso. She is a South African,' I said.

'Girls and boy, we have a mystery to solve,' I told them.

‘Let’s meet at the library during lunchtime and work together to find out more information. We will need to get this mysterious key back to its owner.’ I was determined to solve the mystery of the lost key.

We met at the library during lunch to find out more about Nombuso and how her golden key was lost in Ghana.

Afua researched facts about where she had lived. Mpume searched for information about her family. Thatho and I researched the golden key in general.

Time flew by as we enjoyed doing the research. All of a sudden, the bell rang. Lunch was over already. We were so glued to our research that we didn’t notice the clock ticking.

We agreed to meet at my house after school once we had our parents’ permission. Afua, Mpume and Thatho agreed to ask their parents if we could meet at my house after we’d finished with our house chores.

Time seemed to move as slow as a snail when we got back to class. My mind was not in the lesson at all. I just wanted to get home to figure out The Mystery of the Lost Golden Key with the ‘NK & AK’ initials.

At last, the bell shrieked, marking the end of the day and bringing me back from my daydreaming. I packed up my things and ran out of the door and straight home so quickly that my feet felt as if they were floating on air.

When I got home, I greeted Mum and Dad as I entered the front room before running upstairs, changing and coming back downstairs to finish my chores.

'What's the rush? Slow down, young missy,' Dad said, lifting his eyes away from his computer when he saw me slide past his office.

'Sorry, Dad. I just want to get my chores done on time because Afua, Mpume, Thatho and I have a project we have to work on, and they will be coming over so we can work on it,' I explained as I went out the door to feed the goats and chickens.

Mum gave me a 'what-are-you-kids-up-to-now-look'. It's a look that carries a million words.

'Don't worry, Mum. We are not going to get into trouble,' I said.

Interesting Discovery

My friends came over not long after I'd done my chores. We were eager to share our findings and crack The Mystery of the Lost Golden Key.

'Okay, people, what do we have?' I asked. It was hard to contain my enthusiasm.

'Ama, you will never believe what I found out,' Thatho said with anticipation in his voice and her eyes wide open.

'Go on. Tell us,' we all said together, sounding like a choir.

'Well, Nombuso happens to be my great-grandmother.'

'Really?' we all said.

'Yes. You know my family came from South Africa,' Thatho said.

We all stared at Thatho, shocked but delighted and intrigued.

'When I got home, I told my mum about the project to ask permission to come over to your house, and she was overwhelmed with tears of joy. She told me she had the key and has been looking for it since she lost it when she went to the market on Saturday.'

'Hold on—are you telling us that the key belongs to your family?' Mpume said, a confused look on her face.

'If it belongs to your family, why would your mum carry it with her to the market? It looks too valuable, and it's not just a normal key,' Afua added, seeming to challenge Thatho's story.

'Okay, people, wait a minute, relax, and take in a deep breath,' I said.

'If truly this key belongs to your family, then your mum will be able to tell us more about Nombuso, the original owner, and what the key is for.' I said this in an effort to calm the situation.

'This may mean that we are close to solving the mystery. What do you guys think?' I asked.

Thatho stood up and took out a picture from his pocket. 'My mum gave me this to show you.' He handed the picture to me. It was a picture of a heart-shaped locket and a treasure box. On the treasure box were the same initials as the key with the same, special, cursive writing. We were all astonished.

'Mum has invited you all to come over on Saturday so she can tell us the story of the mysterious key. Please, bring the key with you so we can all see the treasure my great-grandma left in the treasure box,' Thatho said, relaying his mother's invitation.

Wow! This had turned out to be a real adventure. To think I'd found the key to my friend's family treasure. I couldn't wait for the weekend. We were all keen to see the treasure the mysterious golden key would reveal.

Thoughts flooded my mind. Would it be gold, jewellery, diamonds, or a map to a family secret? Was Nombuso a rich woman who had left her fortune in the treasure box? Maybe I would get a share of the gold for finding the key.

My imagination was running away from me.

The Mystery of the Lost Key Unveiled

The weekend came, and I was so excited to go to Thatho's house to see where the golden key might lead. I had told my mum and dad about The Golden Key Project and our findings, and we all got ready to go to Thatho' s house to find out more about the treasures behind the mysterious golden key.

When we got to the house, Mpume and Afua came along with their parents. It was like a private party or a family get-together. Thatho and his parents welcomed us with warm greetings and led us to the front room.

My eyes popped open when I saw the bright golden box on the table with its sparkling shine.

'Akwaaba' Thatho's mum said, and we went to our seats.

'I welcome you all to our home,' Mrs Kwarteng, Thatho's mum, said to greet us.

'Today is a very exciting day for us all as we celebrate the unveiling of our family's treasure. Thank you, Ama, for finding our lost key,' she said with a calm voice.

I looked at her and smiled while holding my dad's hand.

'I am sure you are here to learn more about the mysterious key. Well, let me not waste any more of your time. The key belonged to my husband's grandmother, who was called Nombuso—yes, a South African. I am sure you're asking yourself how it got to Ghana. Well, Nombuso was married to a Ghanaian called Abeiku Kwarteng, and together, they built a family legacy, bringing communities together with their childcare setting across the world.

Their motto was "Encouraging children to achieve their best while having fun". They achieved this by bringing people together from different backgrounds to achieve diversity, love and justice, but most importantly, their foundation in God was their key inspiration.

'Throughout their years and travels, they collected things that will be cherished treasures, not only to generations of their family but the community and the world at large. Their love was inspirational to many, especially those coming from totally different backgrounds and cultures, with the challenge of finding common grounds and overcoming difficult times and oppositions to build a family legacy. In this box is the treasure Abeiku and Nombuso Kwarteng left for us to continue the legacy. The box was sent to our family two weeks ago, but the key was sent separately last Saturday. I went to the post office near the market to pick it up, but unfortunately, it slipped out of my pocket on my way home.'

Thatho's mum's story left us all amazed and overwhelmed. I couldn't believe my ears. The story was out of this world. It was like being in those mystery TV shows.

'Thank you, Ama, for finding the key. We are truly grateful.' With that, she ended the story.

I stood up and gave her the golden key, anxiously waiting to see the treasure inside the box.

Come on, open it, was all I could think while I waited.

The Most Precious Treasure

Mr and Mrs Kwarteng stood up together to make their way to the table on which the box had been placed. They stood on each side of the box. Thatho's mum handed over the key to her husband, who took it, but before he opened it, he looked at everyone. All eyes were glued to the key in his hand. Judging by the look on everyone's faces, we were all nervous but excited to find out what was in the box.

'Before I open the treasure box, I want to say thank you to Almighty God for giving us this opportunity to come together and celebrate this precious moment. Additionally, I want to thank Ama, Afua, Mpume and Thatho for the research leading to the key's coming back to our family. This simply shows the power of friendship and teamwork.'

That being said, he set about to open the box.

We were all sitting on the edge. Even our parents were intrigued as to what was in the box.

Once it was opened, we saw that there was a book, pictures, letters and a golden, heart-shaped locket with sparkling diamonds on it inside.

'Oh,' I said. I couldn't help but express my disappointed expression. 'Where is the treasure?' I asked.

Mrs Kwarteng looked at me with love in her eyes and said, 'This is the treasure,' as she picked up a note from the box and read it aloud.

‘To our family.

‘Here, in this box, is the greatest treasure of all.

‘One is a Bible, to remind you, my beautiful family, that our foundation is built on God, and that is the most important in all you do: let God’s words direct your path. Proverbs 3:5-6 says,” Trust in the Lord with all your heart and lean not on your own understanding. In all your ways submit to him and he will make your path straight,” and remember Philippians 4:13: “You can do all things through Christ who strengthens you.”

‘Two: pictures of family. This is a reminder that family is important. Remember to keep the family bond always. Yes, it will be difficult at times. You will face challenges but do not forget where you come from. Do not abandon your family, and try your best to keep the family unity and peace.

‘Three: letters. These are communications between family members. Remember, communication is key. Take the time to appreciate and talk to each other.

‘Four: the family locket, depicting family on both sides. Inside the locket, our Ghanaian and South African heritage come together as one. Let us keep the bond of unity and add to the locket.

‘These are the greatest treasures in life.’

Everyone in the room cried tears of joy and gratitude. They all stood up and gave Mr and Mrs Kwarteng a round of applause. We all got to have a look at the family treasure. Mrs Kwarteng opened the golden, heart-shaped locket, which had pictures of all family members from Nombuso's South African family and Abeiku's Ghanaian family coming together as one big family. This was the precious treasure: family and love that brings unity and peace.

We were all astonished by the abundance of the family treasure in the box, but my eyes gazed upon something shiny at the bottom of the treasure box, and I wondered what it could be. As it wasn't my box, I held back from picking it up, quietly approaching Mr Kwarteng instead. I cleared my throat and said, 'Please, what's that shiny thing at the bottom of the box?' I pointed at it.

Everyone seemed to have examined the box several times, but no one noticed anything until I pointed it out.

'Ooh, yes. It seems as if there is something we missed,' Mr Kwarteng said, picking up the shiny object.

Maybe this is the real *treasure, just like the movies,* I wondered.

A Treasure Hunt Adventure

Mr Kwarteng picked up the object, a golden envelope sealed with a candle wax stamp into which the initials NK & AK had been pressed.

All eyes were on the envelope, holding everyone's attention.

Mr Kwarteng opened the envelope carefully as we all waited, wondering what could possibly be inside. When he was done, Mr Kwarteng took out a piece of paper from the envelope.

Afua, Mpume, Thatho, and I shrugged our shoulders, disappointed. Not another letter. We all hoped for something of material value inside.

Once Mr Kwarteng had opened the letter, his eyes looked up as if surprised, and he let out a slight shriek of excitement.

'What is it?' Mrs Kwarteng asked, looking over to see what it was.

'It's a map,' Mr Kwarteng said.

'A map!' I said.

'Yes, a map leading us to a location,' Mr Kwarteng replied, still looking shocked and slightly out of breath.

'The instruction simply says, "Work together in unity, and you will find the treasure. The key word is UNITY".'

We let out shouts of excitement. 'Yes!' I said, 'a real treasure hunt.'

'Can we all come with you?' I asked, sounding calm despite my excitement.

'Of course, you can. As the letter said, we must work together in unity. Without all of you, we wouldn't have found the key leading us on this adventure. We will all need to work together to find the last piece of the puzzle.' Mrs Kwarteng said, inviting all of us in the room to join in the adventure.

The map instructed us to go to Winneba in Ghana's central region. We all packed our bags and prepared ourselves for the quest, each of us thrilled and eagerly anticipating the journey.

Unlocking the Treasure

The road trip was full of enjoyment as we played games, occasionally stopping to enjoy the beautiful sites and fruit of the land.

We finally made it to our destination. Mr Kwarteng led the way, giving us directions as he followed the instructions on the map. We worked together in unity as instructed by the letter, helping one another as we climbed hills and went through the maze. We had to be careful and attentive, as one could easily get lost in the maze.

We finally made it to a silver brick wall, which looked like drawers in a dresser, and we had to work together, like a connected chain, to find the loose brick on which the NK & AK initials were embossed in that special cursive writing.

When we found the brick, Mr Kwarteng touched it with the golden key and used his hand to push on the marked brick. All of a sudden, a secret door opened, revealing a cave behind the wall. I was flabbergasted. Everyone's eyes opened widely, their jaws dropping until they'd almost reached the floor.

'Wow,' we all said, astonished at the sight of what stood before us.

We held each other's hands and entered the cave. With every step taken, a new room opened to reveal more treasure inside. In the middle of the cave was a huge chair decorated with precious ornaments and another treasure box sitting on it, only this time, it was covered with sparkling ornaments.

We all went to the box as one as instructed by the letter, and Mr Kwarteng opened the box with the golden key I'd found.

Inside the treasure box was a second, small, navy box. I wondered what was inside, and I said softly, 'What is in the lovely little box, Mr Kwarteng?' He opened it, and inside was a ring with the inscription, 'Abeiku and Nombuso love you from mortality to immortality.'

With tears in his eyes, Mr Kwarteng explained that the ring had been given to Nombuso by her husband, Albert. It was a ring that had belonged to Thatho's great-great-grandmother. It was said that she had been given the ring by her dad, who was a merchant. He had purchased the ring from a sailor and promised to give it to his child should God bless him with one. Thatho's great-great-grandmother decided to keep it safe for a time at some point in the future when her family and other people could work together in unity to unveil such treasure, which belonged in the museum, to demonstrate the power of teamwork.

The box also contained a bracelet with beautiful carvings on it and studded with diamonds. On it was the inscription, 'Love always wins.'

This was, indeed, true. We'd had a great adventure and found real treasure that

Love Always Wins
Love Always Wins

showed us the value of love, unity and peace.

We couldn't wait to get back to school to share our adventure and the values we'd learnt with everyone. As I said at the beginning of this story, it was the most adventurous week of my life.

Ultimately, the values learnt by all members of our four families were the greatest treasures we could share, and we aimed to spread the message to our communities and the world at large so it would have an impact for generations to come.

THE END

Acknowledgements

I wish to express my gratitude and thanks to everyone who worked with me to publish my stories. Firstly, God Almighty for showing me that I can do all things through Christ who strengthens me; my parents, Albert and Nozipho Kittoe; my sister Mary Kittoe for inspiring me; my cousins for always challenging me; my mentor Daniella Blechner and the entire Conscious Dreams Publishing team; all my teachers who have nurtured my writing and A2Zi Childcare for inspiring me with the strength of diversity, inclusion, and equity.

About the Author

Step aside, world, because here comes Sarah Kittoe, an 11-year-old powerhouse who juggles more talents than a circus act (and probably has better jokes, too!). Don't be misled by the Year 7 title–this young lady has already published a whopping four books, proving that age is just a number when you have imagination in your pockets and a pen in your hand.

Sarah's not just a literary whiz. When she's not weaving worlds of words, you'll find her creating masterpieces with art and crafts, designing cool stuff, rocking out to music, crunching numbers like a math whiz, and even playing different sports. Yes, you read that right: this girl is basically a dynamite with a serious case of awesome.

Where does all this inspiration come from? Well, for starters, she's a bookworm who devours stories the way some people inhale pizza. Her imagination is fuelled by playing with her equally fantastic sister, Mary, and sharing the joy of words with the kids at A2Zi Childcare.

Sarah's not just all fun and games (though, trust me, they're pretty fun!). She has a big heart and a passion for helping those in need. Whether it's volunteering her time, raising awareness for important causes or donating money raised, this young lady believes in making the world a better place, and making a positive difference.

Other Books by Sarah Kittoe

If you enjoyed this book, you can get more awesome books written by Sarah and dive into a world of adventure, friendship and mystery

Keep up-to-date with Sarah's journey at www.sarahkittoe.co.uk

Find out more about Sarah's books at www.sarahkittoe.co.uk

TikTok @_sarahkittoebooks

@sarahkittoebooks

Sarah Kittoe

www.sarahkittoe.co.uk

Conscious Dreams
PUBLISHING

Transforming diverse writers into successful published authors

www.consciousdreamspublishing.com

authors@consciousdreamspublishing.com

Let's connect

Milton Keynes UK
Ingram Content Group UK Ltd.
UKHW050234290324
440347UK00002B/17